SPENDING TIME WITH GOD

DEVOTIONALS

Marlene Ellis

All scripture quotations are taken from the King James Version of the Holy Bible and the Perry Stone Hebraic Prophetic Study Bible (New Testament) King James Version.

TABLE OF CONTENTS

The Almighty God....................1

Jesus Christ Our Lord..............6

God's Promises.....................12

Angels.............................18

The Love of God....................22

The Holy Spirit....................28

The Grace of God...................34

Salvation..........................38

Thankful...........................42

Sin................................45

Forgiveness........................49

Faith..............................53

Hope...............................59

Peace..............................63

Anxious............................67

Afraid..........................70

Bereaved......................74

Doubt..........................77

Defeated......................80

Healing........................83

Discouraged..................88

Hatred.........................92

Loneliness....................96

Troubled......................100

The Power OF Prayer.............104

The Blessings of God.............108

The Devil......................112

Marriage......................117

Divorce.......................121

Temptation...................126

Worried.......................129

Vengeance....................132

Wisdom..............................134

Judgment..........................139

Death................................142

Resurrection......................145

Heaven.............................148

Hell...................................152

The Last Days....................156

The Word of God (Bible).........162

INTRODUCTION

Spending time with God is imperative as we face each and every day in a world where perilous times have come. **Matthew 14:10** And then shall many be offended, and shall betray one another and shall hate one another.

As we face so much hatred we must remember that God is in control of this world. He spoke it into existence. He created man in His own image and every person in this life has a purpose.

God loved us even before we were born. He told Jeremiah, Before I formed you in the womb I knew you. Before you were born I sanctified you, I ordained you a prophet to the nations.

The Bible tells us that God is love. He demonstrates His love toward us, in that while we were sinners, Christ died for us. **Romans 5:8** God gave His only begotten Son to give us eternal life and redeem us from our sins.

Now is the time for the harvest. God tells us to work in His fields so that lost souls will be saved. It's His desire that all be saved. The Lord is coming soon to get His Bride, to get those who are watching and praying for His appearance.

So many people are hurting. Problems have invaded their lives. There's a great need to turn to God for help.

The scriptures in this book should be helpful to you, whatever your needs might be, God has the answer.

Spend more time with God by praying, reading His word, studying His word, obeying, loving, serving and worshiping Him.

THE ALMIGHTY GOD

God is for me, Jesus is with me, the Holy Spirit is in me, the Angels are all around me and the devil is under my feet.

He is Jehovah Jireh, God will provide.

He is Jehovah Shalom, God our peace.

He is Jehovah Tsidkenu, God our righteousness.

He is Jehovah Sabaoth, God of hosts.

He is Jehovah Shammah, God is present.

He is Jehovah Elyon, God most High.

I Peter 1:16 Because it is written, Be ye holy, for I am holy.

THE ALMIGHTY GOD

Genesis 1:1 In the beginning God created the heaven and the earth.

Genesis 1:27 So God created man in His own image, in the image of God created He him; male and female created He them.

Genesis 1:28 And God blessed them and God said unto them; Be fruitful and multiply, and replenish the earth, and subdue it; and have dominion over the fish of the sea, and over the fowl of the air, and over every living thing that moveth upon the earth.

THE ALMIGHTY GOD

I John 4:7 Beloved, let us love one another; for love is of God, and every one that loveth is born of God and knoweth God.

John 4:24 God is a Spirit and they that worship Him must worship Him in spirit and truth.

Matthew 12:50 For whosoever shall do the will of my Father, which is in heaven, the same is my brother, and sister, and mother.

John 15:12 This is my commandment, that ye love one another, as I have loved you.

THE ALMIGHTY GOD

I John 4:4 Ye are of God, little children, and have overcome them; because greater is he that is in you, than he that is in the world.

James 4:7 Submit yourselves therefore to God. Resist the devil, and he will flee from you.

James 4:8 Draw nigh to God, and He will draw nigh to you. Cleanse your hands, ye sinners; and purify your hearts, ye double minded.

Romans 8:31 What shall we then say to these things? If God be for us, who can be against us.

THE ALMIGHTY GOD

Romans 8:28 And we know that all things work together for good to them that love God to them who are the called according to His purpose.

Mark 12:30 And thou shalt, love the Lord thy God with all thy heart, and with all thy soul, and with all thy mind, and with all thy strength; this is the first commandment.

Genesis 17:1 I am the almighty God, walk before me, and be thou perfect.

Revelation 19:6B For the Lord God omnipotent reigneth.

JESUS CHRIST OUR LORD

He is the Son of God
He is the mighty King
He is the Holy Savior
He is my precious friend
He's Alpha and Omega
the beginning and the end
His name is Jesus Christ our Lord
He is my everything

JESUS CHRIST OUR LORD

Matthew 1:21 And she shall bring forth a son, and thou shalt call his name Jesus; for he shall save his people from their sins.

Matthew 1:22 Now all this was done, that it might be fulfilled which was spoken of the Lord by the prophet saying.

Matthew 1:23 Behold, a virgin shall be with child, and shall bring forth a son, and they shall call his name Emmanuel, which being interpreted is, God with us.

JESUS CHRIST OUR LORD

Luke 4:18 The Spirit of the Lord is upon me, because he hath anointed me to preach the gospel to the poor; he hath sent me to heal the brokenhearted, to preach deliverance to the captives and recovering of sight to the blind, to set at liberty them that are bruised.

Philippians 2:9 Wherefore God also hath highly exalted him and given him a name which is above every name.

Philippians 2:10 That at the name of Jesus every knee should bow, of things in heaven, and things in earth, and things under the earth.

JESUS CHRIST OUR LORD

Philippians 2:11 And that every tongue should confess that Jesus Christ is Lord, to the glory of God the Father.

John 1:12 But as many as received him, to them gave he power to become the sons of God, even to them that believe on his name.

Romans 8:16 The Spirit itself beareth witness with our Spirit; that we are the children of God.

Romans 8:17 And if children, then heirs; heirs of God, and joint heirs with Christ; if so be that we suffer with him, that we may be also glorified together.

JESUS CHRIST OUR LORD

Luke 24:46 And said unto them Thus it is written, and thus it behoved Christ to suffer, and to rise from the dead the third day.

John 14:6 Jesus saith unto him, I am the way, the truth, and the life; no man cometh unto the Father, but by me.

Colossians 3:1 If ye then be risen with Christ, seek those things which are above, where Christ sitteth on the right hand of God.

JESUS CHRIST OF LORD

Galatians 3:28 There is neither Jew nor Greek, there is neither bond nor free, there is neither male nor female; for ye are all one in Christ Jesus.

Hebrews 12:2 Looking unto Jesus, the author and finisher of our faith; who for the joy that was set before him endured the cross, despising the shame, and is set down at the right hand of the throne of God.

Hebrews 13:8 Jesus Christ the same yesterday, and to day, and for ever.

GOD'S PROMISES

You promised me eternal life
A home in heaven, a robe of white
You promised me eternal joy
And peace within
You promised me eternal bliss
If I'd obey your holy will
I love you Lord with all my heart
My soul, my mind and my strength

Genesis 8:22 While the earth remaineth. seedtime and harvest, and cold and heat, and summer and winter, and day and night shall not cease.

GOD'S PROMISES

Genesis 9:11 And I will establish my covenant with you, neither shall all flesh be cut off any more by the waters of flood, neither shall there any more be a flood to destroy the earth.

Genesis 12:1 Now the Lord had said unto Abram, Get thee out of thy country, and from thy kindred, and from thy father's house, unto a land that I will shew thee.

Genesis 12:2 And I will make of thee a great nation, and I will bless thee, and make thy name great; and thou shalt be a blessing.

GOD'S PROMISES

Genesis 12:3 And I will bless them that bless thee, and curse thim that curseth thee; and in thee shall all families of the earth be blessed.

Genesis 13:14 And the Lord said unto Abram, after that Lot was separated from him, lift up now thine eyes, and look from the place where thou art northward and southward, and eastward, and westward:

Genesis 13:15 For all the land which thou seest, to thee will I give it, and to thy seed for ever

GOD'S PROMISES

Hebrews 10:16 This is the covenant that I will make with them after those days, saith the Lord, I will put my laws into their hearts, and in their minds will I write them;

Hebrews 10:17 And their sins and iniquities will I remember no more.

Ephesians 6:2 Honor thy father and mother; this is the first commandment with promise;

Ephesians 6:3 That it may be well with thee, and thou mayest live long on the earth.

GOD'S PROMISES

Hebrews 11:11 Through faith also Sara herself received strength to conceive seed, and was delivered of a child when she was past age, because she judged him faithful who had promised.

Genesis 35:10 And God said unto him, thy name is Jacob, thy name shall not be any more Jacob, but Israel shall be thy name: and he called his name Israel.

Genesis 35:12 And the land which I gave Abraham and Isaac, to thee I will give it, and to thy seed after thee will I give the land.

GOD'S PROMISES

Acts 2:33 Therefore being by the right hand of God exalted, and having received of the Father the promises of the Holy Ghost, he hath shed forth this which ye now see and hear.

Acts 2:38 Then Peter said unto them, Repent, and be baptized every one of you in the name of Jesus Christ for the remission of sins, and ye shall receive the gift of the Holy Ghost.

Acts 2:39 For the promise is unto you, and to your children, and to all that are afar off, even as many as the Lord our God shall call.

ANGELS

The angels encampeth round about me
I can feel their presence everywhere
When danger appears
The angels are near
To protect me and keep me in their care
They're with me through the day and the night
They wake me to see the morning light
I will never fear,
For they're always near
Yes, the angels encampeth round about me.

ANGELS

Revelation 12:7 And there was war in heaven; Michael and his angels fought against the dragon; and the dragon fought and his angels.

Luke 22:43 And there appeared an angel unto him from heaven, strengthening him.

Luke 4:10 For it is written, He shall give his angels charge over thee, to keep thee.

Luke 15:10 Likewise, I say unto you there is joy in the presence of the angels of God over one sinner that repenteth.

ANGELS

Matthew 28:3 And behold there was a great earthquake for the angel of the Lord descended from heaven, and came and rolled back the stone from the door, and sat upon it.

Matthew 22:30 For in the resurrection they neither marry, nor are given in marriage, but are as the angels of God in heaven.

Revelation 14:6 And I saw another angel fly in the midst of heaven, having the everlasting gospel to preach unto them that dwell on the earth, and to every nation, and kindred, and tongue and people.

ANGELS

Mark 13:32 But of that day and that hour knoweth no man, no not the angels which are in heaven, neither the Son, but the Father.

Jude 6 And the angels which kept not their first estate, but left their own habitation, he hath reserved in everlasting chains under darkness unto the judgment of the great day.

I Peter 3:22 Who is gone into heaven, and is on the right hand of God: angels and authorities and powers being made subject unto him.

THE LOVE OF GOD

I fell in love with the master
many years ago
Since the time that love's done
nothing but grow and grow
He gave me peace, He gave me joy
He put the love in my heart
He took all my sins away
And He gave me a brand new start.

I Corinthians 13:13 And now abideth faith, hope, charity, these three; but the greatest of these is charity.

THE LOVE OF GOD

Romans 8:28 And we know that all things work together for good to them that love God, to them who are the called according to his purpose.

John 3:16 For God so loved the world, that he gave his only begotten Son, that whosoever believeth in him should not perish, but have everlasting life.

I John 4:19 We love him, because he first loved us.

THE LOVE OF GOD

Matthew 22:37 Jesus said unto him, thou shalt love the Lord thy God with all thy heart, and with all thy soul, and with all thy mind.

Matthew 22:38 This is the first and great commandment.

Matthew 22:39 And the second is like unto it, thou shalt love thy neighbor as thyself.

Proverbs 3:12 For whom the Lord loveth he correcteth, even as a father the son in whom he delighteth.

THE LOVE OF GOD

John 15:13 Greater love hath no man than this; that a man lay down his life for his friend.

John 15:14 Ye are my friends, if ye do whatsoever I command you.

John 14:23 Jesus answered and said unto him, If a man love me, he will keep my words; and my Father will love him, and we will come unto him, and make our abode with him.

I John 2:15 Love not the world, neither the things that are in the world. If any man love the world, the love of the Father is not in him.

THE LOVE OF GOD

I John 4:7 Beloved, let us love one another: for love is of God, and every one that loveth is born of God and knoweth God.

I John 4:8 He that loveth not knoweth not God, for God is love.

I John 4:9 In this was manifested the love of God toward us, because that God sent his only begotten Son into the world, that we might live through him.

I John 4:10 Herein is love, not that we loved God, but that he loved us, and sent his Son to be the propitiation for our sins.

THE LOVE OF GOD

I John 4:11 Beloved, if God so loved us, we ought also to love one another.

I John 4:12 No man hath seen God at any time. If we love one another, God dwelleth in us, and his love is perfected in us.

I John 4:18 There is no fear in love; but perfect love casteth out fear; because fear hath torment. He that feareth is not made perfect in love.

I John 4:21 And this commandment have we from him, that he who loveth God love his brother also.

THE HOLY SPIRIT

The spirit came from up above
The spirit came from Jesus' blood
The spirit came in the form of a dove
The spirit came from God's own love
The spirit came at Pentecost
After they were filled
With the Holy Ghost
The spirit came like we were told
It sat upon a hundred twenty souls.

Galatians 5:22 & 23 But the fruit of the Spirit is love, joy, peace, long suffering, gentleness, goodness, faith, meekness, temperance, against such there is no law.

THE HOLY SPIRIT

Genesis 1:2 And the earth was without form and void; and the darkness was upon the face of the deep. And the Spirit of God moved upon the face of the waters.

Genesis 6:3 And the Lord said, My spirit shall not always strive with man, for that he also is flesh yet his days shall be an hundred and twenty years.

Romans 8:6 For to be carnally minded is death; but to be spiritually minded is life and peace.

THE HOLY SPIRIT

Acts 2:38 Then Peter said unto them, Repent, and be baptized every one of you in the name of Jesus Christ for the remission of sins, and ye shall receive the gift of the Holy Ghost.

Acts 2:39 For the promise is unto you, and to your children, and to all that are afar off, even as many as the Lord our God shall call.

Acts 2:4 And they were all filled with the Holy Ghost, and began to speak with other tongues, as the Spirit gave them utterance.

THE HOLY SPIRIT

I Thessalonians 5:23 And the very God of peace sanctify you wholly, and I pray God your whole spirit and soul and body be preserved blameless unto the coming of the Lord Jesus Christ.

Matthew 12:32 And whosoever speaketh a word against the Son of man, it shall be forgiven him: but whosoever speaketh against the Holy Ghost, it shall not be forgiven, neither in this world, neither in the world to come.

Ephesians 4:30 And grieve not the holy Spirit of God whereby ye are sealed unto the day of redemption.

THE HOLY SPIRIT

Romans 8:9 But ye are not in the flesh, but in the Spirit, if so be that the Spirit of God dwell in you. Now if any man have not the Spirit of Christ, he is none of his.

Acts 10:38 How God anointed Jesus of Nazareth with the Holy Ghost and with power; who went about doing good, and healing all that were oppressed of the devil; for God was with him.

Romans 8:14 for as many as are led by the Spirit of God, they are the sons of God.

THE HOLY SPIRIT

John 14:26 But the comforter, which is the Holy Ghost, whom the Father will send in my name, he shall teach you all things, and bring all things to your remembrance, whatsoever I have said unto you.

I Corinthians 2:10 But God hath revealed them unto us by his Spirit for the Spirit searcheth all things, yea, the deep things of God.

I Corinthians 2:14 But the natural man receiveth not the things of the Spirit of God; for they are foolishness unto him: neither can he know them because they are spiritually discerned.

THE GRACE OF GOD

He bore the shame of my sins
When He prayed in agony
When they mocked and beat and stripped Him
When they nailed Him to the tree
He bore the shame of my sins
when He died at Calvary
When He shed His precious blood
By his grace I've been set free

THE GRACE OF GOD

II Corinthians 12:9 And he said unto me, My grace is sufficient for thee: for my strength is made perfect in weakness. Most gladly therefore will I rather glory in my infirmities, that the power of Christ may rest upon me.

Ephesians 2:8 For by grace are we saved through faith, and that not of yourselves, it is the gift of God.

Ephesians 2:9 Not of works, lest any man should boast.

Titus 3:7 That being justified by his grace, we should be made heirs according to the hope of eternal life.

THE GRACE OF GOD

James 4:6 But He giveth grace. Wherefore He saith, God resisteth the proud and giveth grace unto the humble.

Romans 6:14 For sin shall not have dominion over you, for ye are not under the law, but under grace.

Hebrews 4:16 Let us therefore, come boldly unto the throne of grace, that we may obtain mercy, and find grace to help in time of need.

I Timothy 1:14 And the grace of our Lord was exceeding abundant with faith and love which is in Christ Jesus.

THE GRACE OF GOD

Ephesians 1:6 To the praise of the glory of his grace, wherein he made us accepted in the beloved.

Ephesians 1:7 In which we have redemption through his blood, the forgiveness of sins, according to the riches of his grace.

I Corinthians 15:10 By the grace of God I am what I am; and his grace which was bestowed upon me was not in vain; but I laboured more abundantly than they all: yet not I, but the grace of God which was with me.

SALVATION

He died at Calvary

On a cross one blessed day

He shed His precious blood,

His life He freely gave

To give us salvation

So we could live again

He arose from grave you see

He's coming back for you and me

Romans 10:13 for whosoever shall call upon the name of the Lord shall be saved.

SALVATION

Acts 4:12 Neither is there salvation in any other for there is none other name under heaven given among men, whereby we must be saved.

Romans 10:9 That if thou shalt confess with thy mouth, the Lord Jesus, and shalt believe in thine heart that God hath raised him from the dead, thou shalt be saved.

Romans 10:10 For with the heart man believeth unto righteousness; and with the mouth confession is made unto salvation.

SALVATION

Romans 8:32 He that spared not his own Son, but delivered him up for us all; how shall he not with him also freely give us all things?

Acts 16:31 And they said, Believe on the Lord Jesus Christ, and thou shalt be saved, and thy house.

Romans 5:8 But God commendeth his love toward us, in that, while we were yet sinners, Christ died for us.

SALVATION

Acts 3:19 Repent ye therefore, and be converted that your sins may be blotted out, when the times of refreshing shall come from the presence of the Lord.

Hebrews 5:9 And being made perfect, he became the author of eternal salvation unto all them that obey him.

Psalm 62:7 In God is my salvation and my glory: the rock of my strength, and my refuge, is in God.

Psalm 103:12 As far as the east is from the west, so far hath he removed our transgressions from us.

THANKFUL

When trouble comes and
Ole Satan tries to change me
I use the weapon of prayer
to see me through
I call upon my precious
holy, loving Saviour
I'm thankful for the one
I know will see me through
I have thanksgiving in my heart today
I have a joy no one can take away
I am so thankful, Lord
For what you've done for me
You've changed my life
And made me happy as can be.

THANKFUL

Psalm 100:4 Enter into his gates with thanksgiving and into his courts with praise: be thankful unto him, and bless his name.

Psalm 105:1 O give thanks unto the Lord, call upon his name; make known his deeds among the people.

Psalm 105:2 Sing unto him, sing psalms unto him; talk ye of all his wondrous works.

I Thessalonians 5:18 In every thing give thanks for this is the will of God in Christ Jesus concerning you.

THANKFUL

Hebrews 13:15 By him therefore let us offer the sacrifice of praise to God, continually, that is the fruit of our lips giving thanks to his name.

Philippians 4:6 Be careful for nothing, but in every thing by prayer and supplication with thanksgiving let your requests be made known unto God.

Matthew 11:25 At that time Jesus answered and said, I thank thee, O Father, Lord of heaven and earth because thou has hid these things from the wise and prudent, and hast revealed them unto babes.

SIN

I once lived in sin had no peace within
But He put me on my knees
And his power got hold of me
I can sing and shout today
And I'm glad I'm on my way
To a place prepared for me
there my Savior I will see.
He made me free, He made me free
He made me free from the curse of sin, He put new life in me
I don't have to be a part
of the world of sin and shame
He put peace and joy in me
This old person's not the same.

SIN

Romans 3:23 For all have sinned and come short of the glory of God.

I John 1:9 If we confess our sins, he is faithful and just to forgive us our sins and to cleanse us from all unrighteousness.

Romans 6:14 For sin shall not have dominion over you: for ye are not under the law, but under grace.

James 4:17 Therefore to him that knoweth to do good, and doeth it not, to him it is a sin.

SIN

Psalm 85:2 Thou hast forgiven the iniquity of thy people, thou hast covered all their sin Selah

I Samuel 15:23 For rebellion is as the sin of witchcraft, and stubbornness is as iniquity and idolatry. Because thou hast rejected the word of the Lord, he hath also rejected thee from being king.

Romans 12:21 Be not overcome of evil, but overcome evil with good.

Romans 14:16 Let not your good be evil spoken of.

SIN

Isaiah 1:18 Come now, and let us reason together saith the Lord; though your sins be as scarlet, they shall be white as snow, though they be red like crimson, they shall be as wool.

James 4:7 Submit yourselves therefore to God. Resist the devil, and he will flee from you.

James 4:8 Draw nigh to God, and he will draw nigh to you. Cleanse your hands ye sinners; and purify your hearts ye double minded.

Hebrews 8:12 For I will be merciful to their unrighteousness, and their sins and their iniquities will I remember no more.

FORGIVENESS

Father forgive them for they know not
what they do
These were the words of my Savior
As He died for me and you
Every drop of blood that fell
From the cross onto the ground
Every drop was shed by Jesus
So the lost could all be found.
The blood he shed for you and me
Has made the victory oh so sweet
We've been washed by his blood
We've been set free
At Calvary our sins he bore,
Now he's alive forever more
And he said, Father forgive them
For they know not what they do.

FORGEVENESS

Ephesians 4:32 And be ye kind one to another; tenderhearted, forgiving one another, even as God for Christ's sake hath forgiven you.

Psalm 85:2 Thou hast forgiven the iniquity of thy people, thou hast covered all their sin. Selah

Psalm 32:1 Blessed is he whose transgression is forgiven, whose sin is covered.

Colossians 1:14 In whom we have redemption through his blood even the forgiveness of sins.

FORGIVENESS

Matthew 12:32 And whosoever speaketh a word against the Son of man, it shall be forgiven him but whosoever speaketh against the Holy Ghost, it shall not be forgiven him, neither in this world, neither in the world to come.

I John 1:9 If we confess our sins, he is faithful and just to forgive us our sins, and to cleanse us from all unrighteousness.

Colossians 3:13 Forbearing one another, and forgiving one another. If any man have a quarrel against any; even as Christ forgave you, so also do ye.

FORGIVENESS

Matthew 18:21 Then came Peter to him, and said, Lord, how oft shall my brother sin against me. And I forgive him? Till seven times?

Matthew 18:22 Jesus saith unto him, I say not unto thee, until seven times; but, until seventy times seven.

Jeremiah 33:8 And I will cleanse them from all their iniquity, whereby they sinned against me; and I will pardon all their iniquities, whereby they have sinned, and whereby they have transgressed against me.

FAITH

Speak to the mountain
When you're in need
Remove those doubts
Cast them into the sea
God knows your heart
He'll meet your needs
Have faith in God
Just trust Him and believe.
Jesus healed the brokenhearted
The oppressed and the blind
He cast out demons of every kind
He made the lame to walk
Raised the dead from the grave
Have faith in Him
He's still our healer today.

FAITH

Romans 10:17 So then faith cometh by hearing, and hearing by the word of God

I Corinthians 2:5 That your faith should not stand in the wisdom of men, but in the power of God.

Galatians 3:9 So then they which be of faith are blessed with faithful Abraham

Hebrews 11:6 But without faith it is impossible to please him: for he that cometh to God must believe that he is and that he is a rewarder of them that diligently seek him.

FAITH

Hebrews 11:3 Through faith we understand that the worlds were framed by the word of God, so that things which are seen were not made of things which do appear.

Hebrews 11:29 By faith they passed through the red sea as by dry land which the Egyptians assaying to do were drowned.

Ephesians 2:8 For by grace are we saved through faith; and that not of yourselves: it is the gift of God.

II Corinthians 5:7 For we walk by faith, not by sight.

FAITH

Matthew 21:21 Jesus answered and said unto them, Verily I say unto you, If ye have faith, and doubt not, ye shall not only do this which is done to the fig tree, but also if ye shall say unto this mountain, Be thou removed, and be thou cast into the sea, it shall be done.

Matthew 21:22 And all things, whatsoever ye shall ask in prayer, believing, ye shall receive.

James 2:26 For as the body without the spirit is dead, so faith without works is dead also.

FAITH

Luke 18:8 *I tell you that he will avenge them speedily. Nevertheless when the Son of man, cometh, shall he find faith on the earth.*

Ephesians 6:16 *Above alll, taking the shield of faith, wherewith ye shall be able to quench all the fiery darts of the wicked.*

Acts 3:16 *And his name through faith in his name hath made this man strong, whom ye see and know: yea, the faith which is by him hath given him this perfect soundness in the presence of you all.*

FAITH

I Timothy 6:12 *Fight the good fight of faith, lay hold on eternal life, whereunto thou art also called, and hast professed a good profession before many witnesses.*

II Timothy 4:7 *I have fought a good fight, I have finished my course, I have kept the faith.*

II Timothy 4:8 *Henceforth there is laid up for me a crown of righteousness, which the Lord, the righteous judge, shall give me at that day; and not to me only, but unto all them also that love his appearing.*

HOPE

I'm looking for that blessed hope

Of the appearing of our Lord

The glorious appearance of the Great God And our Lord Jesus Christ

Who gave himself for us

That He might redeem us from our sins

I'm looking for that blessed hope

I'm going home to be with him.

Titus 2:13 *Looking for that blessed hope, and the glorious appearing of the great God and our Saviour Jesus Christ.*

HOPE

Titus 2:14 Who gave himself for us, that he might redeem us from all iniquity, and purify unto himself a peculiar people, zealous of good works.

Titus 3:7 That being justified by his grace, we should be made heirs according to the hope of eternal life.

I Corinthians 13:13 And now abideth faith, hope, charity, these three, but the greatest of these is charity.

I Corinthians 15:19 If in this life only we have hope in Christ, we are of all men most miserable.

HOPE

I Corinthians 15:20 But now is Christ risen from the dead, and become the first fruits of them that slept.

II Corinthians 1:7 And our hope of you is steadfast, knowing, that as ye are partakers of the sufferings, so shall ye be also of the consolation.

Galatians 5:5 For through the spirit wait for the hope of righteousness by faith.

Ephesians 1:18 the eyes of your understanding being enlightened that ye may know what is the hope of his calling; and what the riches of the glory of his inheritance in the saints.

HOPE

I Thessalonians 5:8 But let us, who are of the day, be sober, putting on the breastplate of faith and love and for an helmet, the hope of salvation.

Hebrews 11:1 Faith is the substance of things hoped for, the evidence of things not seen.

I Peter 1:3 Blessed be the God and Father of our Lord Jesus Christ, which according to his abundant mercy hath begotten us again unto a lively hope by the resurrection of Jesus Christ from the dead

I John 3:3 And every man that has this hope in him purifieth himself; even as he is pure.

PEACE

Lord I have an inner peace
no one can see
I have that love and compassion
You've given me
Money can't buy it, you freely gave it to me
It will last me a lifetime
It's an everlasting peace

Philippians 4:7 And the peace of God which passeth all understanding, shall keep your hearts and minds through Christ Jesus

Romans 8:6 for to be carnally minded is death, but to be spiritually minded is life and peace.

PEACE

John 16:33 These things I have spoken unto you, that in me ye might have peace. In the world ye shall have tribulation but be of good cheer; I have overcome the world.

Colossians 3:15 Let the peace of God rule in your hearts, to the which also ye are called in one body; and be thankful.

Hebrews 12:4 Make every effort to live in peace with everyone and to be holy: without holiness no one will see the Lord.

Psalm 34:14 Turn from evil and do good, seek peace and pursue it.

PEACE

Romans 16:20 And the God of peace shall bruise Satan under your feet shortly. The grace of our Lord Jesus Christ be with you. Amen

Philippians 4:9 Those things, which ye have both learned, and received, and heard, and seen in me, do: and the God of peace shall be with you.

John 14:27 Peace I leave with you, my peace I give unto you, not as the world giveth do I give unto you. Let not your heart be troubled, neither let it be afraid.

PEACE

Mark 4:39 And he arose, and rebuked the wind, and said unto the sea, Peace be still. And the wind ceased. And there was a great calm.

Ephesians 2:14 For he is our peace, who hath made both one, and hath broken down the middle wall of partition between us.

II Timothy 2:22 Flee also youthful lusts, but follow righteousness, faith, charity, peace, with them that call on the Lord out of a pure heart.

James 3:28 And the fruit of righteousness is sown in peace of them that make peace.

ANXIOUS

Many times man will disappoint you

He's a friend when things are going right

But when you need someone to help

When you're in trouble

There's one who'll be there by your side

His name is Jesus, Jesus, Jesus

He died on a cross

He died for your sins

His name is Jesus, Jesus, Jesus

He loved us so much

He died for His friends

Psalm 46:1 *God is our refuge and strength, a very present help in trouble.*

ANXIOUS

Psalm 46:11 The Lord of hope is with us; the God of Jacob is our refuge. Selah

I Peter 5:6 Humble yourselves therefore under the mighty hand of God, that he may exalt you in due time.

Romans 8:32 What shall we then say to these things? If God be for us, who can be against us?

I Peter 5:10 But the God of all grace, who hath called us unto his eternal glory by Christ Jesus, after that ye have suffered a while, make you perfect, establish, strengthen, settle you.

ANXIOUS

I Peter 5:7 Casting all your care (anxiety) upon him for he careth for you.

Matthew 11:28 Come unto me, all ye that labour and are heavy laden, and I will give you rest.

Philippians 4:19 But my God shall supply all your need, according to his riches in glory by Christ Jesus.

Ephesians 6:10 Finally, my brethren, be strong in the Lord, and in the power of his might.

Ephesians 6:11 Put on the whole armour of God, that ye may be able to stand against the wiles of the devil.

AFRAID

In the midst of the sea
The ship was tossed about
The wind was blowing strong
The disciples were in doubt
In the fourth watch of the night
They saw him walking on the sea
Jesus saw their fear and said
It is I, be not afraid
It is I, be not afraid
I will save you from all harm
I'll raise you up when you are down
There's no need for alarm
I will always be there with you
No matter what you have to face
So be of good cheer,
It is I be not afraid

AFRAID

II Timothy 1:7 For God hath not given us the spirit of fear; but of power, and of love, and of a sound mind.

Luke 12:27 Consider the lilies how they grow: they toil not, they spin not; and yet I say unto you, that Solomon in all his glory was not arrayed like one of these.

Luke 12:28 If then God so clothed the grass, which is today in the field, and tomorrow is cast into the oven, how much more will be clothe you, O ye of little faith?

AFRAID

Luke 12:19 And seek not ye what ye shall eat, or what ye shall drink, neither be ye of doubtful mind.

Luke 12:30 For all these things do the nations of the world seek after: and your Father knoweth that ye have need of these things.

Luke 12:31 But rather seek ye the kingdom of God; and all these things shall be added unto you.

Luke 12:32 Fear not little flock, for it is your Father's good pleasure to give you the kingdom.

AFRAID

Psalm 34:4 *I sought the Lord, and he heard me, and delivered me from all my fears.*

Matthew 10:28 *And fear not them which kill the body, but are not able to kill the soul but rather fear him which is able to destroy both soul and body in hell.*

Ecclesiastes 12:13 *Let us hear the conclusion of the whole matter: fear God and keep his commandments for this is the whole duty of man.*

Hebrews 13:6 *So that we may boldly say. The Lord is my helper, and I will not fear what man shall do unto me.*

BEREAVED

Sometimes we get so weary
Don't know which way to go
Our burdens get so heavy
And we start feeling low
But I know a man who'll lift you up
A man who loves you so
He'll take your burdens all away
The greatest friend you'll ever know.
When you need a miracle
There's one who cares for you
He'll lead you and direct your path
Make the miracle come true
He'll never ever forsake you
He'll be there until the end
He's the greatest one who ever lived
The truest friend that's ever been

BEREAVED

Psalm 34:18 The Lord is nigh unto them that are of a broken heart: and saveth such as be of a contrite spirit.

Psalm 34:22 The Lord redeemeth the soul of his servants and none of them that trust in him shall be desolate.

Matthew 5:4 Blessed are they that mourn; for they shall be comforted.

Matthew 5:8 Blessed are the pure in heart; for they shall see God.

Psalm 30:5 For his anger endureth but a moment, in his favour is life: weeping may endure for a night, but joy cometh in the morning.

BEREAVED

II Corinthians 1:3 Blessed be God even the Father of our Lord Jesus Christ, the Father of mercies, and the God of all comfort.

II Corinthians 1:4 Who comforted us in all our tribulation, that we may be able to comfort them which are in any trouble, by the comfort wherewith we ourselves are comforted of God.

Revelation 21:4 And God shall wipe away all tears from their eyes; and there shall be no more death, neither sorrow, nor crying, neither shall there be any more pain; for the former things are passed away.

DOUBT

*Reach out and touch
The precious Lord
Reach out and touch him
By faith today
He is the King of glory
The truth, the life, the way
Reach out and touch
The precious Savior today
He's got a miracle for you today
He's got a miracle if you will obey
He'll answer your prayers
Supply your every need
If you'll believe him
You'll surely succeed.*

DOUBT

Matthew 6:26 Behold the fowls of the air, for they sow not, neither do they reap, nor gather into barns; yet your heavenly Father feedeth them. Are ye not much better than they?

Philippinas 4:13 I can do all things through Christ which strengtheneth me.

Philippians 4:4 Rejoice in the Lord alway, and again I say. Rejoice.

John 6:27 Labour not for the meat which perisheth, but for that meat which endureth unto everlastig life which the Son of man shall give unto you for him hath God the Father sealed.

DOUBT

Matthew 21:21 *Jesus answered and said unto them, Verily I say unto you, If ye have faith, and doubt not, ye shall not only do this which is done to the fig tree, but also if ye shall say unto this mountain, Be thou removed and be thou cast into the sea: it shall be done.*

Matthew 21:22 And all things, whatsoever ye shall ask in prayer, believing, ye shall receive.

Luke 11:20 But if I with the finger of God cast out devils, no doubt the kingdom of God is come upon you.

DEFEATED

He knows every hurt
He knows every need
Before I ask him
He knows just what I need
He's the great I am God of Abraham
He's the king of all ages
He holds the world in his hand.
He's my great provider
When I feel defeat
He is my redeemer
He supplies all my needs
He is my peace giver Creator of all
He's the Lion of Judah
The greatest one of all.

DEFEATED

Proverbs 3:5 Trust in the Lord with all thine heart and lean not unto thine own understanding.

Proverbs 3:6 In all thy ways acknowledge him, and he shall direct thy paths.

Romans 8:31 What shall we then say to these things? If God be for us, who can be against us?

Romans 8:37 Nay, in all these things we are more than conquerors through him that loved us.

Philippians 4:4 Rejoice in the Lord always: and again I say, Rejoice.

DEFEATED

Romans 8:28 And we know that all things work together for good to them that love God, to them who are the called according to his purpose.

Ephesians 3:20 Now unto him that is able to do exceeding abundantly above all that we ask or think according to the power that worketh in us.

Isaiah 41:10 Fear thou not, for I am with thee; be not dismayed; for I am thy God; I will strengthen thee; yea I will help thee with the right hand of my righteousness.

HEALING

My healing came from the cross
From the man at Calvary
From the stripes on his back
That he bore for you and me.
By his stripes we are healed
I know it happened just that way
That's why I have the victory
The victory that's here to stay.

Isaiah 53:5 But he was wounded for our transgressions, he was bruised for our iniquities: the chastisement of our peace was upon him; and with his stripes we are healed.

Luke 9:6 And they departed, and went through the towns, preaching the gospel and healing every where.

HEALING

Matthew 10:1 And when he had called unto him his twelve disciples, he gave them power against unclean spirits, to cast them out, and to heal all manner of sickness and all manner of disease.

Matthew 10:7 And as ye go, preach, saying, The kingdom of heaven is at hand.

Matthew 10:8 Heal the sick, cleanse the lepers, raise the dead, cast out devils: freely ye have received, freely give.

HEALING

Matthew 9:29 Then touched he their eyes, saying. According to your faith be it unto you.

Matthew 9:30 And their eyes were opened; and Jesus straitly changed them saying. See that no man know it.

Matthew 9:33 And when the devil was cast out, the dumb spake: and the multitudes marvelled, saying. It was never so seen in Israel.

Peter 2:24 Who His own self bore our sins in His own body on the tree, that we being dead to sins, should live unto righteousness by whose stripes ye were healed.

HEALING

Acts 3:6 then Peter said, Silver and gold have I none; but such as I have give I thee: In the name of Jesus Christ of Nazareth rise up and walk.

Acts 3:7 And he took him by the right hand, and lifted him up: and immediately his feet and ankle bones received strength.

Acts 3:8 And he leaping up stood, and walked, and entered with them into the temple, walking, and leaping, and praising God.

Luke 22:51 And Jesus answered and said, Suffer ye thus far. And he touched his ear and healed him.

HEALING

Matthew 8:13 And Jesus said unto the centurion, Go thy way; and as thou hast believed, so be it done unto thee. And his servant was healed in the selfsame hour.

James 5:16 Confess your faults one to another, and pray one for another, that ye may be healed. The effectual fervent prayer of a righteous man availeth much.

Acts 5:16 There came also a multitude out of the cities round about unto Jerusalem, bringing sick folks, and them which were vexed with unclean spirits, and they were healed every one.

DISCOURAGED

Lord you told me you'd supply all my needs

You said you'd give me a reason to live

You said you'd protect me and keep me so near

lord, I know you'll give me all that I need.

Lord you are my great intercessor

You gave me comfort, joy and peace

You are the one who loved me and chose me

Lord you gave me all that I need.

DISCOURAGED

Matthew 5:11 Blessed are ye, when men shall revile you, and persecute you, and shall say all manner of evil against you falsely, for my sake.

Matthew 5:12 Rejoice and be exceeding glad: for great is your reward in heaven, for so persecuted they the prophets which were before you.

Matthew 5:14 Ye are the light of the world. A city that is set on an hill cannot be hid.

Philippians 4:4 Rejoice in the Lord always; and again I say, Rejoice.

DISCOURAGED

Philippians 3:13 Brethren, I count not myself to have apprehended: but this one thing I do, forgetting those things which are behind, and reaching forth unto those things which are before.

Philippians 3:14 I press toward the mark of the prize of the high calling of God in Christ Jesus.

Psalm 55:22 Cast thy burden upon the Lord, and he shall sustain thee: he shall never suffer the righteous to be moved.

Philippians 4:19 But my God shall supply all your need according to his riches by Christ Jesus.

DISCOURAGED

Hebrews 4:16 Let us therefore come boldly unto the throne of grace, that we may obtain mercy, and find grace to help in time of need.

Philippians 2:15 That ye may be blameless and harmless, the sons of God without rebuke, in the midst of a crooked and perverse nation, among whom ye shine as lights in the world.

Philippians 4:19 My God shall supply all your need according to His riches in glory by Christ Jesus.

Romans 8:37 Yes in all things we are more than conquerors through him that loved us.

HATRED

We're living in a world of trouble and strife
There's no place for hatred in our life
God said, love one another a I have loved you
God told us what he wants us to do
Yes, we must love one another
As God loves me and you

Matthew 5:44 But I say unto you, love your enemies, bless them that curse you, do good to them that hate you and pray for them which despitefully use you, and persecute you.

HATRED

Proverbs 10:12 Hatred stirreth up strifes: but love covereth all sins.

Matthew 6:24 No man can serve two masters, for either he will hate the one, and love the other; or else he will hold to one, and despise the other. Ye cannot serve God and mammon.

Matthew 10:22 And ye shall be hated of all men for my name's sake but he that endureth to the end shall be saved.

John 3:20 For every one that doeth evil, hateth the light, neither cometh to the light, lest his deeds should be reproved.

HATRED

John 7:7 The world cannot hate you; but me it hateth, because I testify of it that the works thereof are evil.

Ephesians 5:29 For no man ever yet hated his own flesh; but nourisheth and cherisheth it, even as the Lord the church.

I John 2:9 He that saith he is in the light, and hateth his brother, is in darkness even until now.

I John 2:11 But he that hateth his brother is in darkness and walketh in darkness, and knoweth not whither he goeth, because that darkness hath blinded his eyes.

HATRED

Proverbs 6:16 These six things doth the Lord hate: yea, seven are an abomination unto him.

Proverbs 6:17 A proud look, a lying tongue, and hands that shed innocent blood.

Proverbs 6:18 An heart that deviseth wicked imaginations, feet that be swift in running to mischief.

Proverbs 6:19 A false witness that speaketh lies, and he that soweth discord among brethren.

I John 4:19 We love him, because he first loved us.

LONELINESS

I never feel alone
When the trials of life come
He helps me and lifts me
Until I overcome
He never forgets me
The mistakes that I make
He always forgives me
His flock he'll never forsake.
He is my good shepherd
Who watches over me
He stands at the door
His protection is free
He's with me at night
He takes away all my fear
I'm one of his flock
He's always so near

LONELINESS

Hebrews 13:5 Let your conservation be without covetousness, and be content with such things as ye have; for he hath said, I will never leave thee, nor forsake thee.

Psalm 23:1 The Lord is my shepherd, I shall not want.

Psalm 23:5 Thou preparest a table before me in the presence of mine enemies; thou anointest my head with oil; my cup runneth over.

Psalm 23:6 Surely goodness and mercy shall follow me all the days of my life; and I will dwell in the house of the Lord for ever.

LONELINESS

Isaiah 41:10 Fear not; for I am with thee: be not dismayed; for I am thy God I will strengthen thee; yea, I will help thee; yea, I will uphold thee with the right hand of my righteousness.

Matthew 14:23 And when he had sent the multitudes away, he went up into a mountain apart to pray; and when the evening was come, he was there alone.

Genesis 2:18 And the Lord God said, it is not good that the man should be alone: I will make him an help meet for him.

LONELINESS

Genesis 2:23 And Adam said, this is now bone of my bones, and flesh of my flesh: she shall be called woman, because she was taken out of Man.

Genesis 2:24 Therefore shall a man leave his father and his mother; and shall cleave unto his wife: and they shall be one flesh.

John 8:16 And yet if I judge, my judgment is true: for I am not alone, but I and the Father that sent me.

Matthew 18:20 For where two of three are gathered in my name, there am I in the midst of them.

TROUBLED

When my burdens get so heavy
I can't bear them
When my problems are so bad
I can't cope
I look up to Jesus, my redeemer
He'll intercede to my Father I know.

I look up to Jesus, my redeemer
He is the one who will answer my plea
He'll hear my prayer and see me through
He'll be my help in time of need
I look up too Jesus, Christ my king.

TROUBLED

Psalm 34:6 This poor man cried, and the Lord heard him, and saved him out of all of his troubles.

Psalm 34:7 The angel of the Lord encampeth round about them that fear him and delivereth them.

Psalm 34:17 The righteous cry and the Lord heareth, and delivereth them out of all their troubles.

Psalm 34:19 Many are the afflictions of the righteous, but the Lord delivereth him out of them all.

II Corinthians 4:8 We are troubled on every side, yet not distressed; we are perplexed, but not in despair.

TROUBLED

John 14:1 Let not your heart be troubled ye believe in God, believe also in me.

John 14:2 In my Father's house are many mansions, If it were not so, I would have told you. I go to prepare a place for you.

John 14:3 And if I go and prepare a place for you, I will come again, and receive you unto myself; that where I am, there ye may be also.

Psalm 46:1 God is our refuge and strength, a very present help in trouble.

TROUBLED

Psalm 46:2 Therefore will not we fear, though the earth be removed and though the mountains be carried into the midst of the sea.

Psalm 46:3 Though the waters thereof roar and be troubled, though the mountains shake with the swelling thereof. Selah

Psalm 37:39 But the salvation of the righteous is of the Lord. He is their strength in the time of trouble.

Psalm 37:40 And the Lord shall help them, and deliver them: He shall deliver them from the wicked, and save them because they trust in him.

THE POWER OF PRAYER

There's only one answer
To every prayer we pray
There's only one answer
To the needs we have each day
The answer is Jesus
And the blood that He shed
To pay for our sins
And to make us whole like Him.
His blood is precious and innocent
It's holy and pure
His blood is royal and loving
It's cleansing and sure
His blood is everything we need
To wash our sins away
Jesus' blood is still working
It's still saving souls today.

THE POWER OF PRAYER

James 5:13 Is any among you afflicted? Let him pray. Is any merry? Let him sing psalms.

James 5:14 Is any sick among you? Let him call for the elders of the church; and let them pray over him, anointing him with oil in the name of the Lord.

James 5:15 And the prayer of the faith shall save the sick, and the Lord shall raise him up; and if he have committed sins, they shall be forgiven him.

I Thessalonians 5:17 Pray without ceasing.

THE POWER OF PRAYER

James 5:16 Confess your faults one to another, and pray one for another, that ye may be healed. The effectual fervent prayer of a righteous man availeth much.

Matthew 5:44 But I say unto you, love your enemies, bless them that curse you, do good to them that hate you, and pray for them which despitefully use you and persecute you.

Matthew 26:41 Watch and pray, that ye enter not into temptation for the spirit indeed is willing, but the flesh is weak.

THE POWER OF PRAYER

Luke 18:1 And he spake a parable unto them to this end, that men ought always to pray, and not to faint.

Luke 21:36 Watch ye therefore, and pray always, that ye may be accounted worthy to escape all these things that shall come to pass, and to stand before the Son of man.

I Timothy 2:8 I will therefore that men pray every where, lifting up holy hands, without wrath and doubting.

Proverbs 15:29 The Lord is far from the wicked, but he heareth the prayer of the righteous.

THE BLESSINGS OF GOD

I'm on my way to heaven
I'm just passing through
Till He calls me home, it will do
I'm getting ready for the day
When we'll hear the trumpet sound
To see the Son of man coming
Then I know I'm heaven bound.
I'm looking for that blessed hope
Of the appearing of our Lord
The glorious appearance of the great
God and our Lord Jesus Christ
Who gave himself for us that He
might redeem us from our sins
I'm looking for that blessed hope
I'm going home to be with him.

THE BLESSINGS OF GOD

Psalm 112:1 Praise ye the Lord. Blessed is the man that feareth the Lord, that delighteth greatly in his commandments.

Psalm 112:2 His seed shall be mighty upon earth; the generation of the upright shall be blessed.

Matthew 25:34 Then shall the King say unto them on his right hand, come ye blessed of my Father, inherit the kingdom prepared for you from the foundation of the world.

Genesis 1:22 And God blessed them saying, Be fruitful, and multiply, and fill the waters in the seas, and let fowl multiply in the earth.

THE BLESSINGS OF GOD

Genesis 12:3 And I will bless them that bless thee, and curse him that curseth thee and in thee shall all families of the earth be blessed.

Genesis 9:1 And God blessed Noah and his sons, and said unto them, Be fruitful and multiply, and replenish the earth.

Proverbs 10:6 Blessings are on the head of the righteous, But violence covers the mouth of the wicked.

Proverbs 10:7 The memory of the righteous is blessed, But the name of the wicked shall not.

THE BLESSINGS OF GOD

Revelation 20:6 Blessed and holy is he that hath part in the first resurrection on such the second death hath no power, but they shall be priests of God and of Christ, and shall reign with him a thousand years.

Revelation 22:7 Behold, I come quickly: blessed is he that keepeth the sayings of the prophecy of this book.

Revelation 22:14 Blessed are they that do his commandments, that they may have right to the tree of life, and may enter in through the gates into the city.

II Corinthians 1:3 Blessed be God even the Father of our Lord Jesus Christ, the Father of mercies, and the God of comfort.

THE DEVIL

The devil will be bound for a thousand years

He'll be chained by an angel you see

He'll cast him in the pit and seal the devil in, there'll be peace on earth and all will be fee

When loosed he will try to deceive

But God wins the battle you see

He'll be cast into the fire tormented evermore, and the saints will rejoice with the Lord.

Revelation 12:9 And the great dragon was cast out, that old serpent, called the Devil, and Satan, which deceiveth the whole world: he was cast into the earth, and his angels were cast out with him.

THE DEVIL

Ephesians 2:2 Wherein in time past ye walked according to the course of this world, according to the prince of the power of the air, the spirit that now worketh in the children of disobedience.

I John 3:8 He that committeth sin is of the devil, for the devil sinneth from the beginning. For this purpose the Son of God was manifested, that he might destroy the works of the devil.

Mark 16:17 These signs shall follow them that believe: in my name they shall cast out devils; they shall speak with new tongues.

THE DEVIL

Malachi 3:11 And I will rebuke the devourer for your sakes, and he shall not destroy the fruits of your ground; neither shall your vine cast her fruit before the time in the field, saith the Lord of hosts.

Revelation 20:1 And I saw an angel come down from heaven, having the key to the bottomless pit and a great chain in his hand.

Revelation 20:2 And he laid hold on the dragon, that old serpent, which is the Devil, and Satan, and bound him a thousand years.

THE DEVIL

Revelation 20:3 And cast him into the bottomless pit, and shut him up, and set a seal upon him, that he should deceive the nations no more, till the thousand years should be fulfilled, and after that he must be loosed a little season.

James 4:7 Submit yourselves therefore to God. Resist the devil and he will flee from you.

James 4:8 Draw nigh to God, and he will draw nigh to you. Cleanse your hands, ye sinners, and purify your hearts ye double minded.

THE DEVIL

Ephesians 6:10 Finally, my brethren, be strong in the Lord, and in the power of his might.

Ephesians 6:11 Put on the whole armour of God, that ye may be able to stand against the wiles of the devil.

Matthew 13:39 The enemy that sowed them is the devil; the harvest is the end of the world, and the reapers are the angels.

Revelation 20:10 And the devil that deceived them was cast into the lake of fire and brimstone, where the beast and false prophet are, and shall be tormented day and night for ever.

MARRIAGE

God created man, breathed in him the breath of life

He created the woman, to be his help meet, to be his wife

God placed a blessing on them

To be fruitful and to multiply

To replenish the earth, to be one flesh and live their life

Genesis 1:27 So God created man in his own image, in the image of God created he him; male and female created he them.

MARRIAGE

Genesis 1:28 And God blessed them, and God said unto them, Be fruitful and multiply and replenish the earth and subdue it; and have dominion over the fish of the sea, and over the fowl of the air and over every thing that moveth upon the earth.

Revelation 2:21 And the Lord God caused a deep sleep to fall upon Adam, and he slept: and He took one of his ribs, and closed up the flesh instead, thereof.

Revelation 2:22 And the rib, which the Lord God had taken from man, made he a woman, and brought her unto the man.

MARRIAGE

Revelation 2:23 And Adam said, This is now bone of my bones, and flesh of my flesh: she shall be called woman because she was taken out of man.

Genesis 2:24 Therefore shall a man leave his father and his mother, and shall cleave unto his wife; and they shall be one flesh.

Hebrews 13:4 Marriage is honorable in all, and the bed undefiled, but whoremongers and adulterers, God will judge.

I Corinthians 7:3 Let the husband render unto the wife due benevolence, and likewise also the wife unto the husband.

MARRIAGE

I Corinthians 7:4 The wife hath not power of her own body, but the husband and likewise also the husband hath not power of his own body, but the wife.

Romans 7:3 So then if, while her husband liveth, she be married to another man, she shall be called an adulteress, but if her husband be dead, she is free from the law; so that she is no adulteress, though she be married to another man.

***I Corinthians 7:14** For the unbelieving husband is sanctified by the wife, and the unbelieving wife is sanctified by the husband, else were your children unclean: but now are they holy.*

DIVORCE

Jesus, He speaks peace to my heart
In my lowest valley, we're never apart
He puts His big arms around me
When I'm in despair
he comforts and loves me
Yes, He always cares.
In every situation, He directs my way
He leads me and guides me
Day after day
He protects me and keeps me
In His sheltering arms
He's the king of the universe
My bright and shining star

DIVORCE

Deuteronomy 24:1 When a man hath taken a wife, and married her, and it come to pass that she find no favour in his eyes, because he hath found some uncleanness in her: then let him write her a bill of divorcement, and give it in her hand, and send her out of his house.

Deuteronomy 24:4 Her former husband, which sent her away, may not take her again to be his wife, after that she is defiled, for that is abomination before the Lord.

Matthew 5:31 It hath been said, Whosoever shall put away his wife, let him give her a writing of divorcement.

DIVORCE

Matthew 5:32 But I say unto you, That whosoever shall put away his wife, saving for the cause of fornication, causeth her to commit adultery; and whosoever shall marry her that is divorced committeth adultery.

I Corinthians 7:10 And unto the married I command, yet not I, but the Lord. Let not the wife depart from her husband.

I Corinthians 7:11 But and if she depart let her remain unmarried, or be reconciled to her husband: and let not the husband put away his wife.

DIVORCE

I Corinthians 7:12 *But to the rest speak I, not the Lord. If any brother hath a wife that believeth not, and she be pleased to dwell with him, let him not put her away.*

I Corinthians 7:13 *And the woman which hath an husband that believeth not, and if he be pleased to dwell with her, let her not leave him.*

I Corinthians 7:14 *For the unbelieving husband is sanctified by the wife, and the unbelieving wife is sanctified by the husband; else were your children unclean, but now are they holy.*

DIVORCE

I Corinthians 7:15 But if the unbelieving depart, let him depart. A brother or sister is not under bondage in such cases: but God hath called us to peace.

I Corinthians 7:27 Art thou bound unto a wife? Seek not to be loosed. Art thou loosed from a wife? Seek not a wife.

I Corinthians 7:28 But and if thou marry, thou hast not sinned; and if a virgin marry, she hath not sinned. Nevertheless such shall have trouble in the flesh: but I spare you.

TEMPTATION

He left His home in heaven
Became a part of the human ways
Our great high priest
Was tempted as we are
And He's in heaven today.

I Corinthians 10:13 There hath no temptation taken you but such as is common to man: but God is faithful, who will not suffer you to be tempted above that ye are able, but will with the temptation also make a way to escape, that ye may be able to bear it.

Luke 4:12 And Jesus answering said unto him, it is said, thou shalt not tempt the Lord thy God.

TEMPTATION

Matthew 26:41 Watch and pray that ye enter not into temptation, the spirit indeed is willing, but the flesh is weak.

Luke 11:4 And forgive us our sins, for we also forgive every one that is indebted to us. And lead us not into temptation, but deliver us from evil.

Hebrews 4:15 For we have not an high priest which cannot be touched with the feeling of our infirmities, but was in all points tempted like as we are, yet without sin.

Hebrews 4:16 Let us therefore come boldly unto the throne of grace, that we may obtain mercy, and find grace to help in time of need.

TEMPTATION

James 1:12 Blessed is the man that endureth temptation; for when he is tried, he shall receive the crown of life, which the Lord hath promised to them that love him.

James 1:13 Let no man say when he is tempted, I am tempted of God: for God cannot be tempted with evil, neither tempteth he any man.

James 1:14 But every man is tempted, when he is drawn away of his own lust, and enticed.

II Peter 2:9 The Lord knoweth how to deliver the godly out of temptations, and to reserve the unjust unto the day of judgment to be punished.

WORRIED

Jesus says, cast your cares on me
For I care for you
And don't be troubled or worried
But lean on me
And I will let my peace rest upon you
You're mine
I'll be with you always
Even until the end of time.

Ephesians 3:20 Now unto him that is able to do exceeding abundantly above all that we ask or think, according to the power that worketh in us.

Philippians 4:4 Rejoice in the Lord alway: and again I say, Rejoice.

WORRIED

John 14:18 *I will not leave you comfortless, I will come to you.*

II Corinthians 12:9 *And he said unto me, My grace is sufficient for thee: for my strength is made perfect in weakness. Most gladly therefore will I rather glory in my infirmities, that the power of Christ may rest upon me.*

I Peter 5:6 *Humble yourselves therefore under the mighty hand of God, that he may exalt you in due time.*

I Peter 5:7 *Casting all your care upon him for he careth for you.*

WORRIED

Matthew 6:33 But seek ye first the kingdom of God, and his righteousness, and all these things shall be added unto you.

Matthew 6:34 Take therefore no thought for the morrow: for the morrow shall take thought for the things of itself. Sufficient unto the day is the evil therefof.

Genesis 8:22 While the earth remaineth, seedtime and harvest, and cold and hot, and summer and winter, and day and night shall not cease.

Philippians 4:19 But my God shall supply all your need according to his riches in glory by Christ Jesus.

VENGEANCE

Vengeance belongs to God
He's the ultimate judge you see
Don't try to take His place
Be patient for others to see
Don't let your anger have it's way
Just focus on God's love
and forgiveness today
He knows how to handle
All of your needs
You just need to pray and believe

Romans 12:19 Dearly beloved, avenge not yourselves, but rather give place unto wrath: for it is written, Vengeance is mine; I will repay, saith the Lord.

VENGEANCE

Nahum 1:2 *God is jealous, and the Lord revengeth; the Lord revengeth, and is furious; the Lord will take vengeance on his adversaries, and he reserveth wrath for his enemies.*

Micah 5:15 *And I will execute vengeance in anger and fury upon the heathen, such as they have not heard.*

Leviticus 19:18 *Thou shalt not avenge, nor bear any grudge against the children of thy people but thou shalt love thy neighbor as thyself: I am the Lord.*

WISDOM

A wise man recognizes his errors
And corrects them right away
He is calm and knows how to handle
Each and every day
He is slow to anger, slow to panic
He celebrates each day without strife
He accepts the word of Lord God Almighty
He'll have eternal life.

Ephesians 10:2 A wise man's heart is at his right hand; but a fools heart at his left.

Ephesians 7:5 It is better to hear the rebuke of the wise, than for man to hear the song of the fools.

WISDOM

Ecclesiastes 10:12 *The words of a wise man's mouth are gracious; but the lips of a fool will swallow up himself.*

I Corinthians 3:18 *Let no man deceive himself. If any man among you seemeth to be wise in this world, let him become a fool, that he may be wise.*

I Corinthians 3:19 *For the wisdom of this world is foolishness with God. For it is written, He taketh the wise in their own craftiness.*

I Corinthians 1:19 *For it is written, I will destroy the wisdom of the wise, and will bring to nothing the understanding of the prudent.*

WISDOM

I Corinthians 1:20 *Where is the wise? Where is the scribe? Where is the disputer of this world? Hath not God made foolish the wisdom of this world?*

I Corinthians 1:21 *For after that in the wisdom of God the world by wisdom knew not God, it pleased God by the foolishness of preaching to save them that believe.*

I Corinthians 1:22 *For the Jew require a sign and the Greeks seek after wisdom.*

I Corinthians 1:23 *But we preach Christ crucified, unto the Jews and a stumbling block, and unto the Greeks foolishness.*

WISDOM

I Corinthians 1:25 Because the foolishness of God is wiser than men; and the weakness of God is stronger than men.

I Corinthians 1:26 For ye see your calling, brethren, how that not many wise men after the flesh, not many mighty, not many noble, are called.

I Corinthians 1:27 But God hath chosen the foolish things of the world to confound the wise; and God hath chosen the weak things of the world to confound the things which are mighty.

WISDOM

Proverbs 10:14 Wise men lay up knowledge: but the mouth of the foolish is near destruction.

Luke 2:52 And Jesus increased in wisdom and stature, and in favour with God and man.

I Corinthians 1:30 But of him are ye in Christ Jesus, who of God is made unto us wisdom, and righteousness, and sanctification and redemption.

I Kings 4:29 And God gave Solomon much wisdom and understanding exceeding and largeness of heart; even as the sand that is on the seashore.

JUDGMENT

Many souls stood before God on that day, The books were opened,

they were judged by their works

The book did say

If their names were not written

In the Lamb's book of life

They could not enter heaven's gates

To obtain eternal life.

I Peter 4:17 For the time is come that judgment must begin at the house of God and if it first begin at us, what shall the end be of them that obey not the gospel of God?

Hebrews 9:27 And as it is appointed unto man once to die, but after this the judgment.

JUDGMENT

Romans 14:10 But why dost thou judge thy brother? Or why dost thou set at nought thy brother? For we shall all stand before the judgment seat of Christ.

Revelation 20:11 And I saw a great white throne, and him that sat on it, from whose face the earth and the heaven fled away, and there was found no place for them.

Revelation 20:12 And I saw the dead, small and great stand before God, and the books were opened and another book was opened, which is the book of life: and the dead were judged out of those things which were written in the books, according to their works.

JUDGMENT

Ephesians 12:14 *God shall bring every work into judgment, with every secret thing, whether it be good, or whether it be evil.*

I John 4:17 *Herein is our love made perfect, that we may have boldness in the day of judgment: because as he is so are we in this world.*

Matthew 12:36 *Every idle word that men shall speak, they shall give account thereof in the day of judgment.*

Revelation 22:12 *Behold, I come quickly; and my reward is with me, to give every man according as his work shall be.*

DEATH

I want to be in a place
Where no fear will enter in
Where there'll be no death or pain
Where there'll be no more sin
Everything will be perfect
That we have to share
Lord, I want to go
Because I know you'll be there.
I want to be there in heaven
With my Savior
With the almighty God
Who died for me
I want to see His loving face and
Hold His precious nail scarred hands
I want to be there with Jesus
In that new and glorious land.

DEATH

Ecclesiastes 7:1 A good name is better than precious ointment, and the day of death than the day of one's birth.

Hebrews 9:27 And as it is appointed unto man once to die, but after this the judgment.

II Corinthians 5:8 We are confident, I say, and willing rather to be absent from the body, and to be present with the Lord.

Proverbs 18:21 Death and life are in the power of the tongue: and they that love it shall eat the fruit thereof.

DEATH

John 11:25 Jesus said unto her, I am the resurrection, and the life: he that believeth in me, though he were dead, yet shall he live.

John 11-26 And whosoever liveth and believeth in me shall never die. Believeth thou this?

Romans 6:23 For the wages of sin is death, but the gift of God is eternal life through Jesus Christ our Lord.

John 10:10 The thief cometh not, but for to steal, and to kill, and to destroy: I am come that they might have life, and that they might have it more abundantly.

RESURRECTION

When the trumpet sounds
The dead in Christ will rise
Then we which are alive
Will meet Jesus in the sky
In a twinkling of an eye
We'll be changed from mortal men
Yes, I know my Lord is coming again

I Corinthians 15:20 But now is Christ risen from the dead, and become the first fruits of them that slept.

I Thessalonians 4:16 For the Lord himself shall descend from heaven with a shout, with the voice of the archangel, and with the trump of God: and the dead in Christ shall rise first.

RESURRECTION

I Thessalonians 4:17 Then we which are alive and remain shall be caught up together with them in the clouds, to meet the Lord in the air: and so shall we ever be with the Lord.

Matthew 22:30 For in the resurrection they neither marry, nor are given in marriage, but are as the angels of God in heaven.

John 5:28 Marvel not at this: for the hour is coming in the which all that are in the graves shall hear his voice.

John 5:29 And shall come forth: they that have done good, unto the resurrection of life; and they that have done evil, unto the resurrection of damnation.

RESURRECTION

II Corinthians 4:14 Knowing that he which raised up the Lord Jesus shall rise up us also by Jesus, and shall present us with you.

Revelation 1:18 I am he that liveth and was dead: and behold, I am alive for evermore. Amen: and have the keys of hell and of death.

Revelation 20:6 Blessed and holy is he that hath part in the first resurrection: on such the second death hath no power, but they shall be priests of God and of Christ, and shall reign with him a thousand years.

HEAVEN

I read about a city
With a wall so great and high
A jasper wall, twelve gates of pearl
Oh what a beautiful sight
The gates of it shall not be shut by
day, there is no night
Where the saved of all the nations
Shall be walking in the light.
The street of the city
As transparent glass, pure gold
Where God almighty and the Lamb
Are the temple I am told
Some day we'll enter in
If our names are written there
In the holy book in heaven
In the Lamb's book of life.

HEAVEN

John 14:2 *In my Father's house are many mansions: if it were not so, I would have told you. I go to prepare a place for you.*

John 14:3 *And if I go and prepare a place for you, I will come again, and receive you unto myself; that where I am, there ye may be also.*

Matthew 7:21 *Not everyone that saith unto me, Lord, Lord shall enter into the kingdom of heaven; but he that doeth the will of my Father which is in heaven.*

Isaiah 55:9 *For as the heavens are higher than the earth, so are my ways higher than your ways, and my thoughts than your thoughts.*

HEAVEN

John 3:3 Jesus answered and said unto him, Verily, verily, I say unto thee, Except a man be born again, he cannot see the kingdom of God.

Matthew 7:13 Enter ye in at the strait gate: for wide is the gate and broad is the way, that leadeth to destruction, and many there be which go in thereat.

Matthew 7:14 Because strait is the gate and narrow is the way, which leadeth unto life, and few there be that find it.

Revelation 21:27 And there shall in no wise enter into it any thing that defileth, neither whatsoever worketh abomination, or maketh a lie: but they which are written in the Lamb's book of life.

HEAVEN

Revelation 22:14 Blessed are they that do his commandments, that they may have right to the tree of life, and may enter in through the gates into the city.

II Peter 3:10 But the day of the Lord will come as a thief in the night; in the which the heavens shall pass away with a great noise, and the elements shall melt with fervent heat, the earth also and the works that are therein shall be burned up.

II Peter 3:13 Nevertheless we, according to his promise, look for new heavens and a new earth, wherein dwelleth righteousness.

HELL

This world is full of sorrows

There's trouble everywhere

Men have failed to serve the Lord

They just don't seem to care

But when I hear the trumpet sound

I'm gonna shout the victory

I'm not getting ready to die

I'm getting ready to live.

Luke 16:22 *And it came to pass, that the beggar died, and was carried by the angels into Abraham's bosom: the rich man also died, and was buried.*

Luke 16:23 *And in hell he lift up his eyes, being in torments, and seeth Abraham afar off, and Lazarus in his bosom.*

HELL

Luke 16:24 *And he cried and said, Father Abraham, have mercy on me, and send Lazarus, that he may dip the tip of his finger in water, and cool my tongue; for I am tormented in this flame.*

Luke 16:25 *But Abraham said, Son remember that thou in thy lifetime receivedst thy good things, and likewise Lazarus evil things: but now he is comforted, and thou art tormented.*

Luke 16:26 *And beside all this, between us and you there is a great gulf fixed: so that they which would pass from hence to you cannot; neither can they pass to us, that would come from hence.*

HELL

Revelation 20:11 And I saw a great white throne, and him that sat on it, from whose face the earth and the heaven fled away; and there was found no place for them.

Revelation 20:12 And I saw the dead, small and great stand before God; and the books were opened: and another book was opened, which is the book of life: and the dead were judged out of those things which were written in the books, according to their works.

Revelation 20:13 And the sea gave up the dead which were in it; and death and hell delivered up the dead which were in them: and they were judged every man according to their works.

HELL

Revelation 20:14 And death, and hell were cast into the lake of fire. This is the second death.

Revelation 20:15 And whosoever was not found written in the book of life was cast into the lake of fire.

Revelation 20:10 And the devil that deceived them was cast into the lake of fire and brimstone, where the beast and false prophet are, and shall be tormented day and night for ever and ever.

Colossians 3:2 Set your affection on things above, not on things on the earth.

THE LAST DAYS

The end is drawing nigh
It may be any day
There's earthquakes wars and rumors
There's a great falling away
We see signs being fulfilled
There's knowledge everywhere
There's trouble home and abroad
Not many seem to care.

Acts 2:17 And it shall come to pass in the last days, saith God, I will pour out of my Spirit upon all flesh: and your sons and your daughters shall prophesy, and your young men shall see visions, and your old men shall dream dreams.

THE LAST DAYS

Acts 2:18 And on my servants and on my handmaidens I will pour out in those days of my Spirit; and they shall prophesy.

Acts 2:19 And I will shew wonders in heaven above, and signs in the earth beneath; blood, and fire, and vapour of smoke.

Acts 2:20 The sun shall be turned into darkness, and the moon into blood, before that great and notable day of the Lord come.

Acts 2:21 And it shall come to pass that whosoever shall call on the name of the Lord shall be saved.

THE LAST DAYS

II Thessalonians 2:3 *Let no man deceive you by any means: for that day shall not come, except there come a falling away first, and that man of sin be revealed, the son of perdition.*

Matthew 24:3 *And as he sat upon the mount of Olives, the disciples came into him privately saying, Tell us, when shall these things be? And what shall be the sign of thy coming, and to the end of the world?*

Matthew 24:4 *And Jesus answered and said unto them, Take heed that no man deceive you.*

Matthew 24:5 *For many shall come in my name saying; I am Christ; and shall deceive many.*

THE LAST DAYS

Matthew 24:6 *And ye shall hear of wars and rumours of wars: see that ye be not troubled: for all these things must come to pass, but the end is not yet.*

Matthew 24:7 *For nation shall rise against nation, and kingdom against kingdom: and there shall be famines, and pestilences, and earthquakes, in divers places.*

Matthew 24:8 *All these are the beginning of sorrows.*

Matthew 24:9 *Then shall they deliver you up to be afflicted, and shall kill you: and ye shall be hated of all nations for my name's sake.*

THE LAST DAYS

Matthew 24:10 And then shall many be offended, and shall betray one another, and shall hate one another.

Matthew 24:11 And many false prophets shall rise, and shall deceive many.

Matthew 24:12 And because iniquity shall abound, the love of many shall was cold.

Matthew 24:13 But he that shall endure unto to end, the same shall be saved.

Matthew 24:14 And this gospel of the kingdom shall be preached in all the world for a witness unto all nations; and then shall the end come.

THE LAST DAYS

II Timothy 3:1 This know also, that in the last days perilous times shall come.

II Timothy 3:2 For men shall be lovers of their own selves, covetous, boasters, proud, blasphemers, disobedient to parents, unthankful, unholy.

II Timothy 3:3 Without natural affection, trucebreakers, false accusers, incontinent, fierce, despisers of those that are good.

II Timothy 3:4 Traitors, heady, highminded, lovers of pleasures more than lovers of God.

II Timothy 3:5 Having a form of godliness, but denying the power thereof: from such turn away.

THE WORD OF GOD (BIBLE)

The word of God is a book of instructions. It's the sword of the spirit. The Bible is holy, sacred, hopeful, loving, precious, anointed, quick, powerful, truthful, real, alive, and infallible.

The word of God speaks to you. It judges, ministers, teaches, blesses, restores, comforts, strengthens, saves, and gives us eternal life.

We need to spend time with God by reading the word, speaking the word, teaching the word, singing the word, living the word, and obeying the word.

THE WORD OF GOD (BIBLE)

Hebrews 4:12 For the word of God is quick, and powerful, and sharper than any twoedged sword, piercing even to the dividing asunder of soul and spirit, and of the joints and marrow, and is a discerner of the thoughts and intents of the heart.

II Timothy 2:15 Study to show thyself approved unto God, a workman that needeth not to be ashamed, rightly dividing the word of truth.

John 5:24 Verily, verily, I say unto you, He that heareth my word, and believeth on him that sent me; hath everlasting life, and shall not come into condemnation; but is passed from death unto life.

THE WORD OF GOD (BIBLE)

Romans 10:17 So then faith cometh by hearing and hearing by the word of God.

II Peter 1:21 For the prophecy came not in old time by the will of man: but holy men of God spake as they were moved by the Holy Ghost.

Hebrews 11:3 Through faith we understand that the worlds were framed by the word of God, so that things which are seen were not made of things which do appear.

THE WORD OF GOD (BIBLE)

Proverbs 13:13 Whoso despiseth the word shall be destroyed: but he that feareth the commandment shall be rewarded.

Isaiah 55:11 So shall my word be that goeth forth out of my mouth. It shall not return unto me void, but it shall accomplish that which I please, and it shall prosper in the thing whereto I sent it.

II Timothy 3:16 All scripture is given by inspiration of God, and profitable for doctrine, for reproof, for correction, for instruction in righteousness.

THE WORD OF GOD (BIBLE)

II Timothy 3:15 And that from a child thou has known the holy scriptures, which are able to make thee wise unto salvation through faith which is in Christ Jesus.

Revelation 22:18 For I testify unto every man that heareth the words of the prophecy of this book. If any man shall add unto these things, God shall add unto him the plagues that are written in this book.

Revelation 22:19 And if any man shall take away from the words of the book of this prophecy, God shall take away his part out of the book of life and out of the holy city, and from the things which are written in this book.

ABOUT THE AUTHOR

Marlene Ellis is a retired Real Estate Broker and County Government employee. She has served the Lord Jesus Christ for over 59 years. She is presently the Minister of Music at the Chapmanville Church of God. Chapmanville, West Virginia. She is also Choir Leader, Soloist, and Representative for Mountaineer Ministries (Home Missions). She has also served as Sunday School Teacher, and Youth Leader.

She enjoys singing, writing and sewing. She has written over 87 gospel songs, some of which she has sung in church. She has compiled several cookbooks. West Virginia Recipes "Country Cookin" was published by Amazon in 2018.

Marlene loves spending time with her family. She has four children, four grandchildren and was married to Ted Ellis, a retired educator and coach, who went home to be with the Lord this year (2020).

Made in United States
Cleveland, OH
12 August 2025